To Lauren and Sarah, the two newest skiers in the family

Library of Congress Cataloging-in-Publication Data
Van Dusen, Chris.
Learning to ski with Mr. Magee / by Chris Van Dusen.
p. cm.
Summary: An encounter with a moose while they are learning to ski
provides Mr. Magee and his dog with some unexpected excitement.
ISBN 978-0-8118-7495-3 (alk. paper)
[1. Stories in rhyme. 2. Skis and skiing—Fiction. 3. Dogs—Fiction.]
I. Title.
PZ8.3.V335Le 2010
[E]—dc22
2009048564

Book design by Kristine Brogno and Rachel Liang.
Typeset in Filosofia.
The illustrations in this book were rendered in gouache.

Manufactured in China.

9 10 8

Chronicle Books LLC
680 Second Street, San Francisco, California 94107

www.chroniclekids.com

Learning to Ski

to Ski

with

Mr. Magee

by Chris Van Dusen

chronicle books·san francisco

One winter morning at 6:53,
Mr. Magee and his little dog, Dee,
Woke to fresh snow and a beautiful sky
And decided, "It's time to give skiing a try!"

"Before we drive all the way up to Mt. Snow,
Follow me, Dee, I know right where to go.
    Across from the house and just up the way
Is a great little hill with a view of the bay.
    We'll practice up there 'til we learn how to ski,
Then we'll head for the mountain," said Mr. Magee.

A few minutes later they came to a spot

Where nothing could get in their way, MaGee thought.

So he put on his skis. Dee hopped in the pack.

And with poles in his hands and his dog on his back

He inched to the edge very slowly until

His skis teeter-tottered, then started downhill!

Not far down the hillside from Mr. Magee,

And just out of sight, there happened to be

A curious moose. He was out on a search

For the succulent sticks of the Great Northern Birch.

Then he spotted a tree. The biggest he'd seen!

On the opposite side of a gaping ravine.

The moose turned around and what did he see?

MR. MAGEE and his little dog, DEE!

The moose was so shocked he stood frozen in fear.

But MR. MAGEE hadn't learned how to steer!

And he knew very soon they were going to collide,

So he called to the moose, "Would you please step aside?!"

But the moose didn't move. So MaGee yelled, "DUCK!"

And that was the moment they ran out of luck.

'Cause while they were sliding right under the moose,

The tips of the skis snagged the log of a spruce!

In a flash and a flip they flew over the log,
Tossing poor Mr. Magee and his dog
Head over heels straight into the gap . . .

When the ends of the skis came down with a slap!

So there they were stranded, Magee and his pup,

Across a ravine, a hundred feet up!

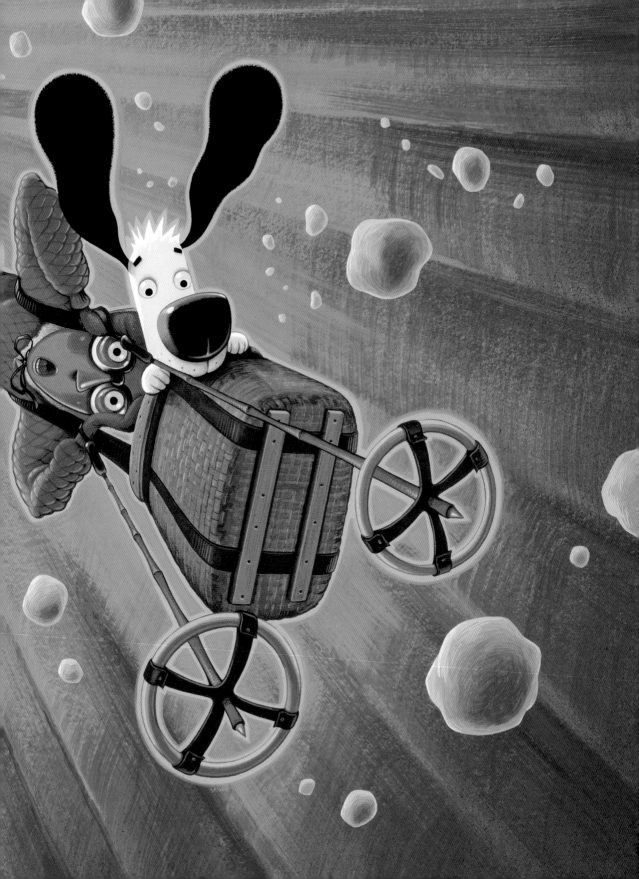

They hung there, suspended, not making a sound.

When the moose came back, he looked all around.

He didn't see DEE or MAGEE—but what's this?

A bridge to the birch above the abyss!

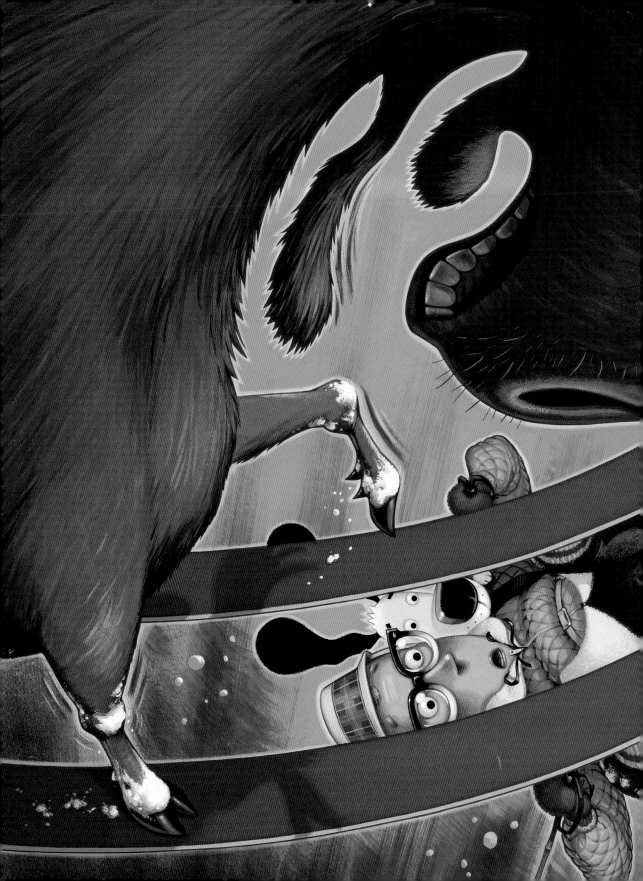

The moose took a step. He was steady and slow,

But his weight caused the skis to sag and to bow.

And when he looked down his heart skipped a beat—

For MR. MAGEE was right under his feet!

With a snort the moose leapt! The skis went SPRING!

They popped in the air with a ZIP and a ZING!

And up like a rocket shot Dee and Magee . . .

Landing feet first just as safe as can be!

"Well, *that* was exciting," said Mr. Magee,
"But I'm not really sure we learned how to ski.
I think that I might need a lesson or two.
I think that, perhaps, it's the best thing to do.
And when we get home," he said with a smile,

"We'll let someone else use the skis for a while."